Boots
for Beth

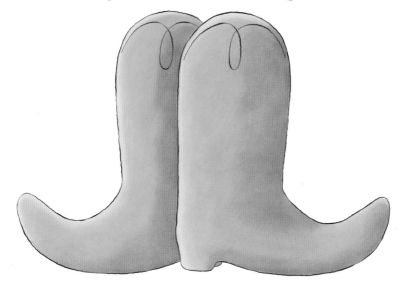

Alex Moran
Illustrated by Lisa Campbell Ernst

Green Light Readers
Harcourt, Inc.
San Diego   New York   London

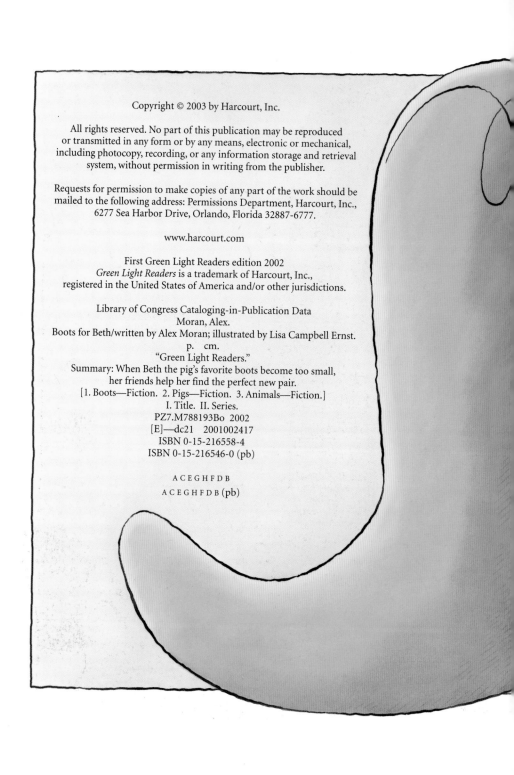

www.harcourt.com

First Green Light Readers edition 2002
Green Light Readers is a trademark of Harcourt, Inc.,
registered in the United States of America and/or other jurisdictions.

Library of Congress Cataloging-in-Publication Data
Moran, Alex.
Boots for Beth/written by Alex Moran; illustrated by Lisa Campbell Ernst.
p.   cm.
"Green Light Readers."
Summary: When Beth the pig's favorite boots become too small,
her friends help her find the perfect new pair.
[1. Boots—Fiction. 2. Pigs—Fiction. 3. Animals—Fiction.]
I. Title. II. Series.
PZ7.M788193Bo 2002
[E]—dc21   2001002417
ISBN 0-15-216558-4
ISBN 0-15-216546-0 (pb)

A C E G H F D B
A C E G H F D B (pb)

Beth was sad.

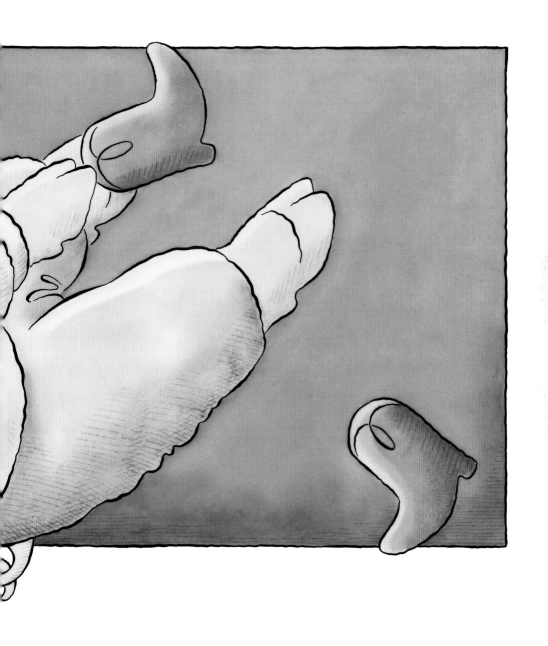

"My red boots don't fit," she cried.
"I cannot get them on."

"Could you use my boots?" asked Meg.

"Too big," said Beth.

"Will my boots fit?" asked Ned.

"Too small," said Beth.

"Could you use my boots?" asked Liz.

"Too soft," said Beth.

"Will my boots help?" asked Ted.

"Too wet," said Beth.

"Can you put on my boot?" asked Jeff.

"Too thin," said Beth.

Beth still felt sad.
Her friends all felt bad.

Then they found a big
surprise for Beth.

"New red boots!" said Beth.
"Thanks."

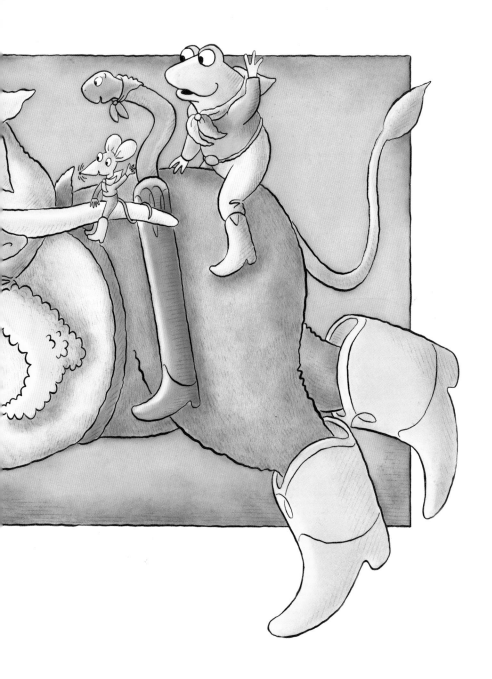

"Now, it's time to play!"
said Beth's friends.

Meet the Illustrator

Lisa Campbell Ernst *got the idea for* Boots for Beth *while shopping for shoes with her two children. "How sad we feel when a favorite pair of shoes no longer fits!" she says. "Then the search for just the right new pair begins. Some shoes are too big, too small, too stiff. At last you find just the right ones!"*

© Vedros & Associates

Lisa Campbell Ernst